This book belongs to:

....

....

GRAFFEG

The Word Bird
published by Graffeg June 2016
© Copyright Graffeg 2016
ISBN 9781910862438

Text © 2016 Nicola Davies.
Illustrations © 2016 Abbie Cameron.
Designed and produced by Graffeg
www.graffeg.com

Graffeg Limited, 24 Stradey Park Business
Centre, Mwrwg Road, Llangennech, Llanelli,
Carmarthenshire SA14 8YP Wales UK
Tel 01554 824000 www.graffeg.com

Graffeg are hereby identified as the authors of
this work in accordance with section 77 of the
Copyrights, Designs and Patents Act 1988.

A CIP Catalogue record for this book is available
from the British Library.

THE WORD BIRD

Written by
Nicola Davies

Illustrated by
Abbie Cameron

Beak and feather,
nest and wing
Flap and Peck and
hop and Sing
They all add up
to Just one word...

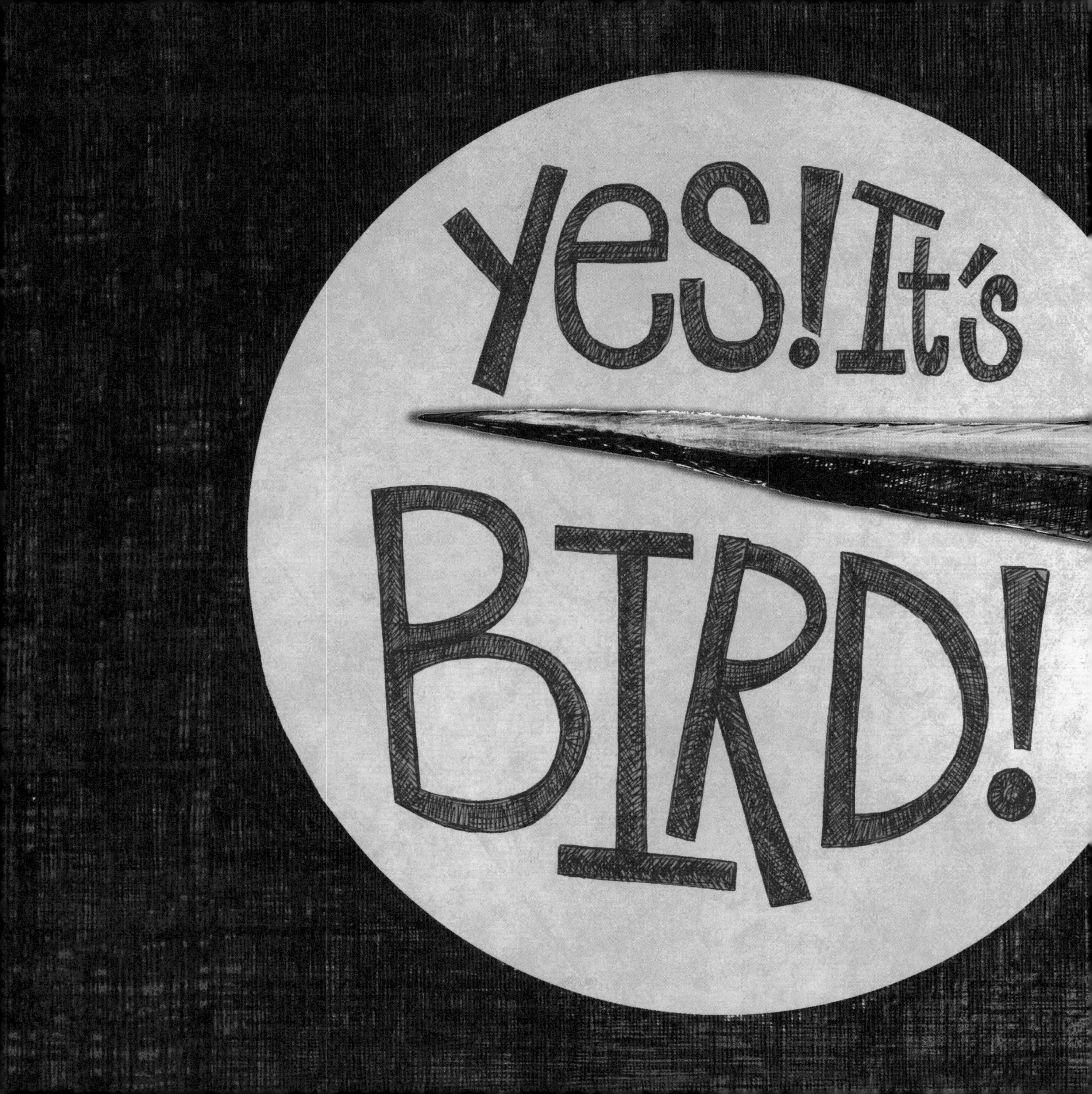
Yes! It's
BIRD!

Teeny tiny, tiny, flitting, round,

Or huge and walking on the ground.

Perching high up in a tree,

or gliding

far, far
out at sea.

Hooting in the darkest night?

All so different but just one word describes them all ...

Beaks that

Sift,

or sew

or grab

And feet that

Paddle,

Cling

Or stab.

Wings for flapping, soaring, swooping

Or underwater loop the looping.

With fancy tails and heads with crests,

With PLUMES and funny blowy blowy UP Chests!

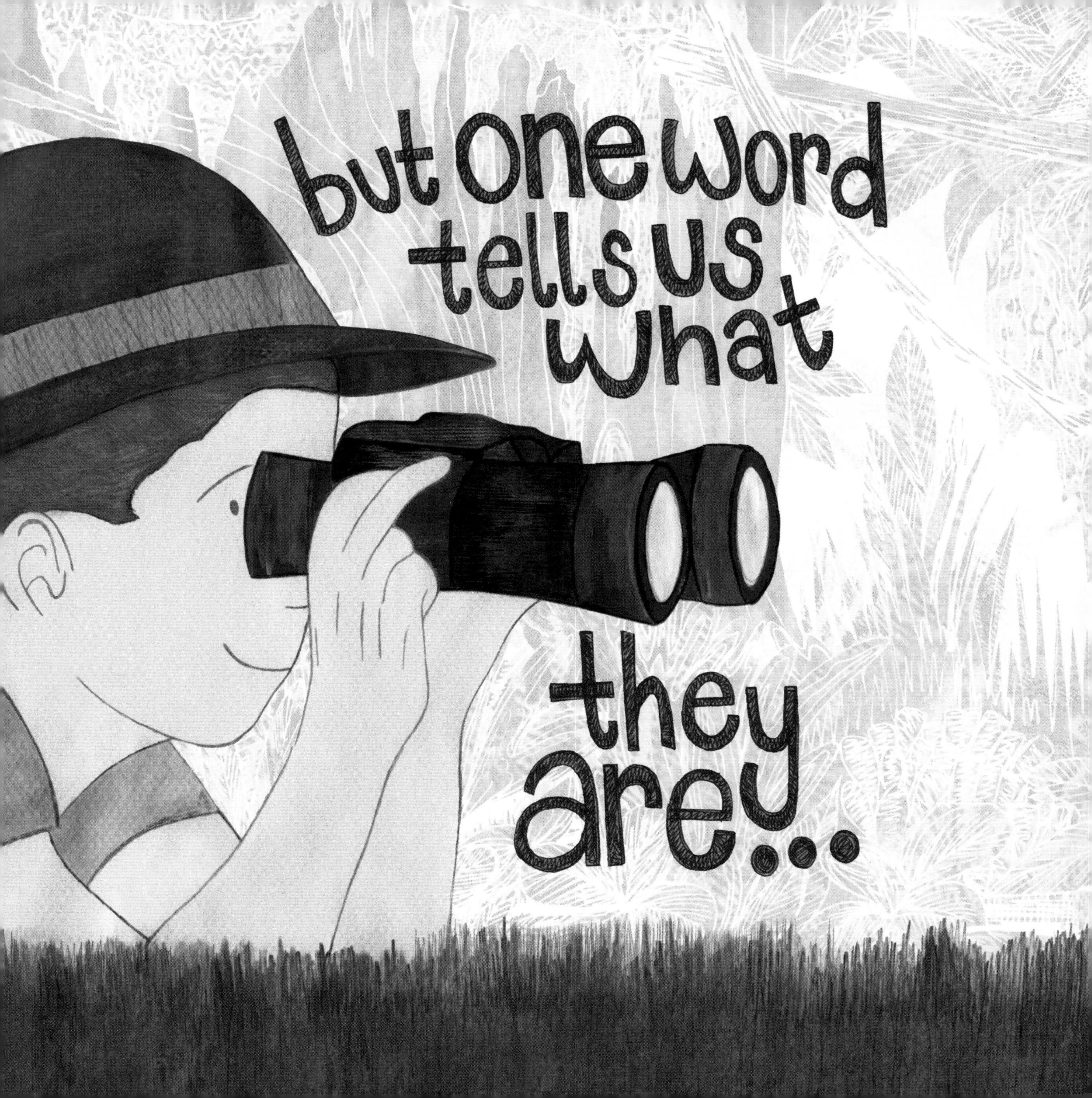
but one word
tells us
what
they
are...

it's

PUZZLE TO FINISH

and now for a little test...
Can you find each bird its nest?

1

2

3

4

5

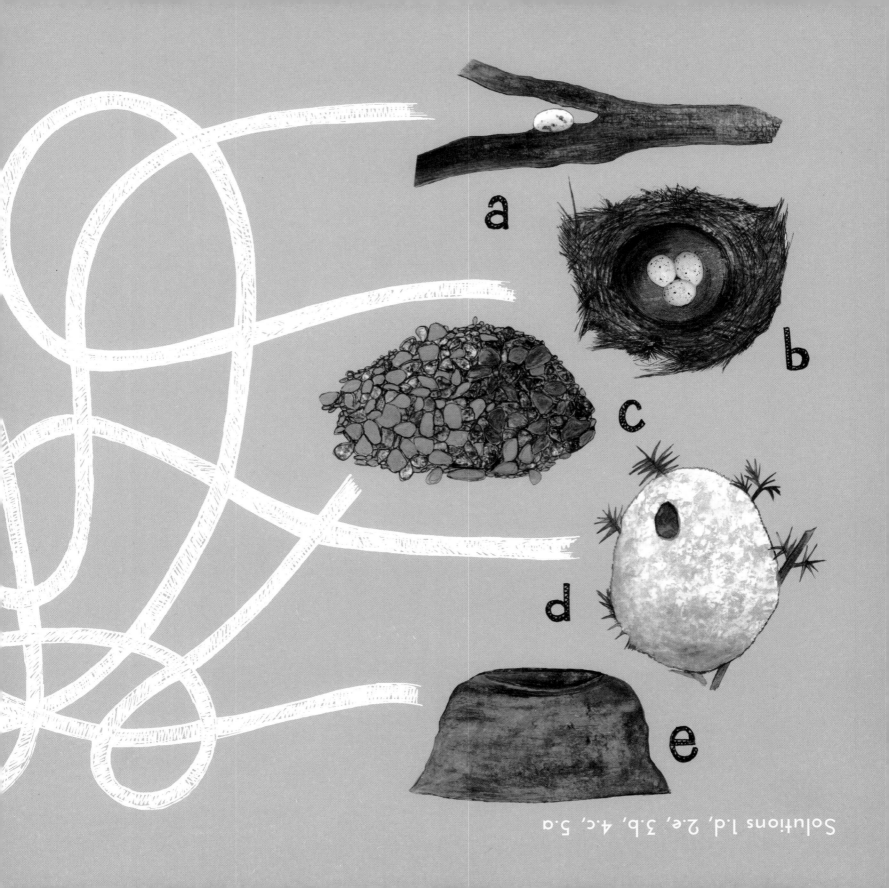

a

b

c

d

e

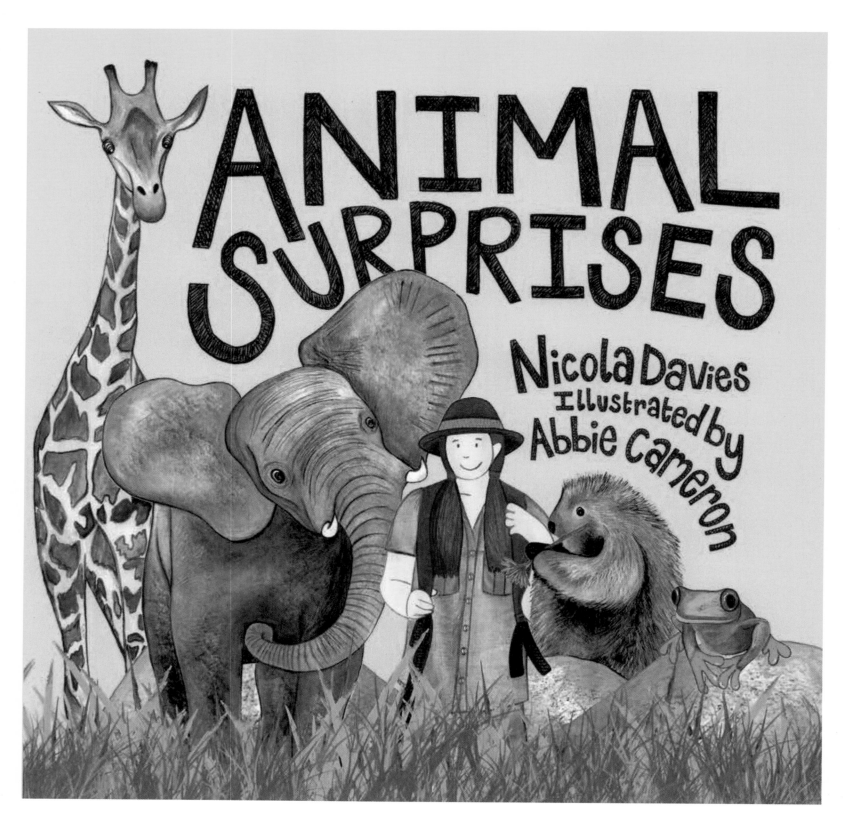

Animal Surprises, also available in this series.

Into The Blue, also available in this series.

Nicola Davies

Nicola is an award-winning author, whose many books for children include *The Promise* (Green Earth Book Award 2015, Greenaway Shortlist 2015), *Tiny* (AAAS Subaru Prize 2015), *A First Book of Nature*, *Whale Boy* (Blue Peter Award Shortlist 2014), and the Heroes of the Wild Series (Portsmouth Book Prize 2014). She graduated in zoology, studied whales and bats and then worked for the BBC Natural History Unit. Underlying all Nicola's writing is the belief that a relationship with nature is essential to every human being, and that now, more than ever, we need to renew that relationship. Nicola's children's books from Graffeg include *Perfect*, the Shadows and Light series, *The Word Bird*, *Animal Surprises* and *Into the Blue*.

Abbie Cameron

Abbie Cameron was raised on the farmlands of the West Country. Surrounded by nature, she developed a love and appreciation for all creatures great and small. Abbie studied Illustration at University of Wales Trinity Saint David, where she first met Nicola Davies. Her style is playful and inventive, sharing some of the tongue-in-cheek attitude and doodle-like style of other contemporary British illustrators. She employs the use of bright colours and texture, whilst playing with scale, composition and open space. *The Word Bird*, *Animal Surprises* and *Into the Blue* are Abbie's first published books but she hopes to continue a career in picture book illustration. Other notable achievements include being short-listed and received highly commented in the Penguin Random House Design Awards 2014.